A Fresh Look At Fairy Tales:

A Thematic Unit
Exploring Gender Bias in Classic Stories

Theda Detlor

SCHOLASTIC
PROFESSIONAL BOOKS

NEW YORK • TORONTO • LONDON • AUCKLAND • SYDNEY

To my sons, Lawrence and Owen

ACKNOWLEDGMENTS

I wish to thank:

Denise Levine, my director at the New York City Lab School at the time I developed this curriculum. Her creativity, intelligence, energy, ideas, encouragement, and belief in me fueled this work.

Kerry Weinbaum, my present director, who has encouraged this work to flourish in new directions.

Judith Pasamanick, director of the NEH Folklore Institute. Her wisdom, spirit, creativity, and belief in me led to the blossoming of my knowledge of folklore and ways to implement this work in the classroom.

Jack Zipes, who was an amazing, generous, and encouraging authority in the areas in which I sought to learn.

My colleagues at the NEH Folklore Institute and at the New York City Lab School, for our great exploratory conversations.

My husband, Len, and sons, Lawrence and Owen, for always being there for me, teaching me, and believing in me.

My parents, Ruth and Sol Rosenbluth, for encouraging me to read and to question.

My patient, supportive, and encouraging editors at Scholastic Professional Books, Terry Cooper and Liza Charlesworth, whose professional and thoughtful comments helped me to shape this book.

My fabulous students, my partners in learning, without whom this work would never have come to be.

Cover design by Vincent Ceci and Jaime Lucero
Interior design by Solutions by Design, Inc.
Cover and interior illustrations by Delana Bettoli
Photos by Lori Aidala unless otherwise indicated

ISBN 0-590-25107-4

Contents

Introduction

As a young child, I loved reading and hearing stories. I remember weekly trips to the library, carrying home as many books as I could and looking forward to being transported to wonderful worlds through those books.

Years later, after discovering the joys and benefits of reading aloud to my sons, I became a teacher. I looked forward to presenting to my young students many of the same stories I knew from my childhood and/or read to my own children. From 1991 on then, as part of a curriculum for my first and second graders, I read aloud many stories to my classes and embarked on a study of the Grimms' fairy tales with them.

The children became especially engrossed in the fairy tales. Each time I opened a book to read a fairy tale aloud, the classroom became quiet and the children's eyes widened. They listened intently as I read. My students had strong responses to the conclusions of these stories, as well. On one occasion they cheered when Gretel out-witted the witch, and, on another, sighed with relief when the shoe slid easily onto Cinderella's foot.

But, what had started as simple read-aloud sessions of Grimms' fairy tales slowly grew into something much deeper as that school year and subsequent years proceed-ed. During the first year with the unit, my class and I enjoyed the stories, discerned their structures, and developed creative projects across the curriculum. But during the next two years, my students and I broadened our perceptions of the tales. We found, to our surprise, a level of gender stereotyping in the tales that needed to be addressed rather than automatically emulated. So, during the next two years, my goals and the lessons I conducted in the unit expanded to address this issue, as well.

In my classroom and throughout this book, teaching critical thinking about sto-ries and the values they might contain became one of my main priorities. Along with improving the children's skills in reading, writing, and other curriculum areas, I want-ed to make boys and girls more consciously aware that there were some strong mes-sages in some stories with which they did not have to agree (all boys are saviors; girls are frail and need assistance from others) and to realize they could write their own tales to change those messages. It became important to me that the children realize they need not and should not necessarily internalize the roles as portrayed in some traditional fairy tales. I wanted children to make choices in their own behavior. I wanted them to know that they need not adhere to rigid gender roles as they go about their lives. I think our study made an impact.

I'm happy to report that the units continued to be a vehicle for many cross-curricular projects, from music to art to dance. This book will describe where and how the fairy tale unit originated, how it developed and branched into other disciplines, and how my students and I changed as a result of our work.

Since teaching is always a work in progress, I plan to use what I have learned to fuel other critical studies with my students. I continue to develop through, and along with, my students. I hope that this book will be a helpful model for you to develop a unit about important issues in your and your students' lives.

Theda's students display their own fairy tales.

CHAPTER 1

The Fairy Tale Unit Emerges

An Initial Fairy Tale Study

The idea for a fairy tale unit came from a child in my class. In 1991, my first graders and I were reading books by author/illustrator Eric Carle. From *A House for Hermit Crab* to *Rooster's Off to See the World*, we pored over Carle's stories and his beautiful collages.

One day, I came across *Treasury of Classic Stories for Children*, a collection of fables and fairy tales that were not authored but selected, retold, and illustrated by Eric Carle.

I began to read these stories to the class and noticed that they were longer, denser, and less obviously structured than those actually authored by Eric Carle. Yet they held my students' attention. In fact, one day, when the whole volume was finished, Heather B. asked, "Can we study more fairy tales?" I happily complied.

I looked through my home library and found *The Complete Fairy Tales of the Brothers Grimm* (translated and with an introduction by Jack Zipes), which I had received as a holiday gift a few years earlier. I brought it to class.

I started reading these stories aloud. Clearly, there were fewer illustrations in this book compared with the Eric Carle books. To visualize the images in the stories, my students had to rely on words rather than pictures. They did that with little difficulty, though. Since their reading and listening skills had progressed throughout the year, they were understanding more complex sentences. The children were well prepared to listen to the longer stories. In fact, they listened with rapt attention.

We began looking at similarities between the stories written by the Grimms—in structure, in types of characters, in characters' behavior. After reading a story aloud, I would encourage this analysis by asking, "How is this tale similar to other fairy tales I read to you?" We talked it over. We discussed how the stories began and ended; how they developed; uses of magic, special numbers, helpers; and how the characters acted overall.

The more fairy tales I read aloud, the more similarities the children noticed. By the time we had finished reading 32 stories in this volume, the children had dictated a useful chart (see page 9).

We would return to the list at a later time.

What We Have Learned About Fairy Tales

1. Fairy tales are stories from a long time ago.
2. They have magical characters.
3. They are not real.
4. Good people have good endings.
5. Bad people have bad endings.
6. Heroes are often kings, queens, princesses, and princes.
7. Villains are witches, monsters, and beasts.
8. Fairy tales use opposites like rich and poor, good and bad, big and little.
9. Fairy tales begin with "Once upon a time..."
10. Fairy tales end happily.
11. Fairy tales are scary in the middle.
12. Many stories were written down by the Brothers Grimm.
13. Many stories teach a lesson.
14. The numbers 3, 7, 12, and 100 are special.
15. Characters often trick each other.
16. Characters who break promises are punished.
17. Characters can die but come back to life.
18. Magical characters are often old.
19. Characters go into the woods to seek their fortunes.
20. Many stories have flowers.
21. Couples want children but have to pay in some way.
22. Wishes are granted.
23. Magic is used to punish.
24. Bears and other animals act like people.
25. People can turn into animals.
26. Animals are helpers.
27. Heroes can help others and then are helped back.
28. Time can pass without change.
29. Things repeat but get bigger.
30. Fairy tales seem to come alive when you read them.

The Seeds of a Fairy Tale/ Gender Issues Curriculum

I was thrilled with my students' developing abilities to discern structure in stories (things repeat and get bigger), to compare (in both stories animals were helpers), and to generalize (the characters often trick each other).

I went on to share with them fairy tales from other sources. Once a friend lent me the picture book *Sir Gawain and the Loathly Lady*, retold by Selina Hastings. The book would have an effect on the direction the unit would take in the future.

In this Arthurian legend, King Arthur is to be put to death by an evil knight unless he can answer the question, "What is it that women most desire?" The answer? "What all women most desire is to have their own way."

I paused midpoint in the story before reaching the answer. What did they think the "answer" might be? With little hesitation, they said that "a woman wants to marry a prince, to be taken care of, and to live happily ever after."

I must admit that, at first, I was dismayed at the stereotypical viewpoint. However, I became consciously aware of this message in the Grimms' tales we had just finished reading. While that notion of women might appear to have been advocated by the Grimms' tales, I now wondered what effect the stories' messages were having on my children today. Times and values have changed. Was I limiting youngsters' aspirations by presenting such tales to the class? If the stories always portrayed women and girls as passive and always portrayed males as active and saviors, was I limiting their views of themselves?

I looked back at the What We Learned About Fairy Tales chart and focused on number 19: "Characters can go into the woods to seek their fortunes." I mentally reviewed the main characters who voluntarily ventured through the woods (as in *Briar Rose* or *Snow White*, for example). For the most part, those characters were males. The female character who strayed off the path in the woods—Little Red Riding Hood—got into trouble and was rescued by a man. I wondered about the effect on youngsters' self-images and aspirations of reading books of this nature.

Realizing the powerful effect literature might have on children's values, I planned to be more aware of the stories' overt and covert messages. If the messages were less than constructive, what should I do?

The Debate Continues

I was of two minds about this. On the one hand, I wanted my children to appreciate the stories. The tales were part of our culture. Barely a day goes by in which I don't hear, see, or read a reference to these tales. Youngsters should be exposed to classic stories like *Briar Rose* and *Little Red Cap*. Furthermore, the stories were interesting, even gripping, with clear beginnings, middles, and endings. And the language of the Grimms' tales was wonderfully rich in clarity and imagery. They would be models for the elements of stories in general. My children could use the stories as models for their own writing.

On the other hand, the stories had potentially negative effects. The sex stereotyping could be damaging. What should I do?

Help Is on the Way

The answer came in the form of work done by two outstanding researchers: Dr. Judith Pasamanick and Dr. Jack Zipes, with whom I worked at the NEH Folklore Institute. Eventually, Dr. Pasamanick taught me ways to use folklore to develop critical thinking skills in children. I was able to continue presenting such literature to the class—for the fun of it, for the love of language—and use the stories to sharpen students' critical thinking skills.

The works of Dr. Jack Zipes were also helpful. As well as translating the Grimms' work, he had written extensively on fairy tales and had explored in his lectures and books the issues of sexism in folktales. What's more, he had compiled an anthology entitled *Don't Bet on the Prince: Contemporary Fairy Tales in North America and England*. It contained "modern" fairy tales, written to confront issues of sexism. His accompanying critical essays focused on fairy tales and their effect on the socialization of children. I read much of his work.

With this research to support me, I now had the resources to carry out a new fairy tale unit with my next class. The unit would use the same intriguing stories, but would also take into account the need for a critical look at some of their limitations. The stories would serve as a foundation for growth for me and my students.

The Time Frame

The following September I started a new unit with my first/second-grade multi-age class. I changed and refined the work further the following year with my next first/second-grade class. The student work samples you'll see on the following pages come primarily from my third year of teaching this unit.

CHAPTER 2

Finding and Critiquing Messages in Stories

The Plan

During the fall semester, I planned to introduce the works of three children's authors: Dr. Seuss, Leo Lionni, and William Steig. Although they did not write folk or fairy tales, I expected to use books by these authors to help children to discover authors' messages and to think critically about those messages. Later, during the spring semester, I planned to introduce the works of the Brothers Grimm. My goals for the spring term would be to help my students apply what they had learned in critical thinking to the Grimms' portrayals of gender roles.

This chapter focuses on my efforts during the fall semester only. The following chapters focus primarily on my efforts during the spring semester.

Taking Off with Dr. Seuss

I chose the beloved Dr. Seuss for many reasons. For one, I knew that his stories—from *And to Think That I Saw It on Mulberry Street* to *Green Eggs and Ham*—had strong appeal to kids. After all, the story lines are fun! Who wouldn't laugh when Horton, an elephant, hatches an egg? What young child wouldn't giggle when the Cat in the Hat comes back? I wanted kids to *like* books, and Dr. Seuss's works were sure to appeal to their sense of silliness and their appreciation of good stories.

In addition, I knew that Dr. Seuss often wrote in rhyme. Through his books, children would develop a sense of the sound of language, especially rhyming words. This would provide a good foundation for their listening skills. Furthermore, the cartoon-like art of Dr. Seuss appeals to children's whimsy. What's more, *I* liked the books!

Of course, I was also aware of the messages—some quite direct—in his books (many are repeated during refrains). Since I planned to teach lessons on authors' messages, starting with a unit on Dr. Seuss seemed most appropriate.

Getting Started

I began by asking children what they already knew about Dr. Seuss and his books. At this point their knowledge was very general. We then developed a chart (see page 15).

Later, we would talk more about his books and the messages they contained.

What Do We Know About Dr. Seuss Books?

1. They are funny.
2. A lot of kids read his books.
3. They have "crazy" pictures.
4. They have jokes and riddles.
5. The words rhyme.

Finding Messages in the Stories

With the children gathered around me in a circle, I read Dr. Seuss books aloud: My class roared at *Hop on Pop*, belly-laughed at *How the Grinch Stole Christmas*, and giggled again with *The Lorax*.

Sometimes I'd read a book a second time. Then I would ask, "What have you noticed?" It was during these discussions that students often commented on the story's message. Once, I read aloud *Horton Hears a Who*. The class noticed the refrain: "...a person's a person no matter how small." I asked students what they thought the refrain meant. "No matter what people look like, they should still be treated equally," they said. To my question "What have you noticed?" first grader Heather answered, "The books have messages." This was the start of children's critical thinking about books.

Before long, I asked the children to think of the messages contained in other Dr. Seuss books. Once, I read aloud *Oh the Places You'll Go*. To my question "What message do you think Dr. Seuss is telling us?" Patrick replied, "Sometimes things don't go the way you hope, but sometimes they do."

I was proud of my children's increasing ability to discern messages. On another occasion, for example, I read aloud *Horton Hatches the Egg*, in which Horton the Elephant promises to stay on Lazy Bird Mayzie's egg until the bird returns. In the end, Horton is rewarded for keeping his promise through thick and thin. In reaction to this story, Danny remarked, "I think the message is that it is important to keep your promise, even when it's hard." (Danny was clearly taking note of the repeating refrain, "I meant what I said and I said what I meant...an elephant's faithful one hundred percent.")

Writing Responses

I often asked youngsters to write a response to a tale, either about the whole story ("That character learned that honesty is better than lying") or a part of it ("I was scared when she entered the forest.") Or the comment could be a thought triggered by the story ("That character reminds me of my brother.")

Initially, the children's comments were short and general. For example, Andi, who later developed into a remarkable writer, wrote of *How the Grinch Stole Christmas*—one of the first I had read aloud—"I liked it because it was nice." But as time went on, responses became more specific. I had taught the class two possible ways to spot a message: by looking at the repeating refrain or by focusing on the ending of the story, which sometimes summarizes the moral. Apparently, the children understood this because, one week after writing "I like it because it was nice," Andi responded to the character Gertrude McFuzz with a message of her own: "You should be happy with what you are. If I saw an elephant, I would not turn into one." Andi had begun to personalize the events in the stories by relating them to how *she* would feel in that character's place. I was encouraged by her growth.

CONNECTIONS TO CHILDREN'S EXPERIENCE

After a while, with each book I would ask the children, "Can you give me an example of this message from your own life?" In response to *McElligot's Pool* Andi wrote, "It reminded me of my two turtles. One of them got sick, and we threw it back where it came from. And my other turtle escaped."

Casey, who initially responded to a Dr. Seuss book by writing, "I liked it," now wrote in response to *The Big Brag*, "It reminded me of my friend. He says, 'I'm better' because he can ride a two wheeler and I ride a training wheeler." The children were growing as readers and writers.

PERSONALIZING MORALS

I became convinced that the children, through reading and discussion, were becoming more deeply invested in the books. They realized that the tales were vehicles for examining and sharing events from their own lives. This was our first step in looking for, and personalizing, authors' messages. The next steps would be to look for more subtle messages in stories and to examine whether the students agreed or disagreed with the messages they found.

Greetings, Leo Lionni!

We were now ready to look at work in which the messages were implied, rather than stated directly. To help achieve that goal, I presented the works of award-winning children's book author Leo Lionni. Lionni writes fables in which the morals are open to interpretation. Reacting to stories such as *Swimmy* or *Fish Is Fish,* children talked about the events and what they mean. They eventually came to the conclusion that these stories, too, have messages. But children disagreed about what those messages were. So on the chart on which I recorded their observations, I wrote: *We are finding different messages in Lionni's books.*

MORE CHALLENGING QUESTIONS

Before long, I ended a read-aloud with a new question. Rather than asking, "What is the message in the story?" I asked, "What do *you* think is the message?" I told students that any answer was acceptable if they could justify it with clear reasons.

In addition, each time children found what they thought was the moral of a story, I asked them to give examples of this moral from their own lives. Here are samples of their written responses to some of Lionni's stories.

Fish Is Fish

> "I think the message is you should help people. Sometimes I help my brother reach the elevator button when he can't reach it."—Casey

> "The moral of this story is we are not the same."—Patrick M.

It is interesting to note that the two children found different meanings in the same story.

Swimmy

Children also found slightly different, but plausible, messages in this tale.

> "It is good to be helping each other."—Patrick M.

> "If you can't do it, ask somebody. It reminds me of when me and my brothers were bringing a bed into the house."—Mark

> "You should all work together."—Danny

While Shayna agreed with Danny's interpretation, she added her own related anecdote:

> "One time my cousin came and we made a mess. Then he didn't want to help me put it back."

Tico and the Golden Wings

"I think the message is it is better to be different than the same. Sometimes I see people that are different and I feel good that I'm different. People are different because they look different or they feel different or they don't have a leg or an arm or they have different dreams."—Andi

"I think the message is that it is important to help one another. The time I helped my friend with her homework, her mom told my dad. Her mom liked it. My dad liked it too. It's important to help her because she's in first grade. She doesn't know very much."—Anju

Tico and the Golden Wings.
Andi
What do you think is the message.
I Think the message is its better to be difrint tlen the same. Give an example in your life. sometimes I see people that are difrint and I feel good that I'm difrikt. People are difrint becavse thay feel difrint and they look difrint or they don't have a lege or an arm and they have difrint dreams.

Frederick

"I think the moral is when you use your imagination you can go anywhere. You can even speak to someone who is dead. When my great grandma died it made me feel sad because I wanted to tell her one last thing but I could not because she died. I miss her. I liked her so, so, so much. She was a great, great grandma. I keep thinking about her in my mind."—Casey

Now that children were personalizing the messages, they began to think about the morals they would like to transmit in their own works. This would alter the way many of my students viewed literature. They now recognized that there is a person "behind" a book.

Choosing a Personal Message

I gave my children a homework assignment. I asked them to make up a moral they would like to teach and then tell why they chose it. My aim was to make them aware that writers often have this motivation for telling stories.

Here are some of the messages my students suggested.

"My moral is that twins are different. I chose that because I am a twin."
—Mark

"When you share something that you have with somebody else, the next time that somebody might share with you. I went apple picking and gave a neighbor some apples. Then she made apple pies and gave some to me."
—Daniel

"Everybody's different. Nobody is the same. I chose this moral because it doesn't matter what you are. Everybody should be treated equally."
—Anju

Constructing Personal Fables

Then I asked each child to construct a fable to illustrate the moral. They could start by answering the following questions.

1. Who are your characters?

2. What problem do they need to solve?

3. How will your story tell your message?

The children used outlines as they wrote. Their fables were then combined to form a class anthology entitled *Oh, Fables!*

Here are samples of their products:

"Once there were four birds. One was ugly. He was named P. J. One was named Holk. One was named Vele. And one was named Axie.

P. J. was lonely. He didn't have any friends. But he was very nice. And the other birds were mean.

One day they were all grown up. Everybody was into girls. So they looked around. They all saw some nice girls. So they went to talk to them. They acted

> Andi
>
> Once there was four birds. One was ugly. He was named PJ. One was named Holk. One was named Vele. And one was named Axie. PJ was very lonely. He didn't have any friends. But he was very nice. And the other birds were mean. One day they were all grown up. Every body was into girls. So they looked around. They all saw some nice girls. So they went to talk to them. They acted mean. So the girls didn't like them. So they dumped them. But they liked PJ. because he was nice inside.
> Moral: It doesn't matter what you look like on the out side it just matters what you look like on the inside.

mean. So the girls didn't like them So they dumped them. But they liked P. J. because he was nice inside.

MORAL: *It doesn't matter what you look like on the outside. It just matters what you look like on the inside."* —Andi

"Once upon a time two cats were walking in the woods when one said, 'My type is smarter.' 'No it isn't! We are all equal.' Then he said, I'll show you." And then he began to fly. And never again did the other tease him.

MORAL: *Everybody has something special about them.* —Christina

> Christina
> Once apon a time 2 cats were walking in the woods when one cat said my type is smarter. No it isn't! We all are equal. Then he said I'll show you. And then he began to fly and naver again did the other tease him.
>
> Moral: Evry-body has something spacial about them.

> by JON.
> A few days ago IN the jungle the monkey teased the giraffe because the Monkey said Oh You have a NECK the monkey didn't want him to get the alpples He got the alpples from his big long NeCk.
>
> Moral: Don't be bothered wheN people tease you.

A few days ago, in the jungle, the monkeys teased the giraffes because the monkey's said, "Oh you have a neck." The monkey didn't want him to get the apples. He got the apples from his big, long neck.

MORAL: *Don't be bothered when people tease you.* —Jon

Introducing Folklore

Now that the children were understanding and identifying with the form of fable in children's literature, I felt it was time to introduce the fable genre in folklore. After I defined folklore for them (a story passed from one teller to another by word of mouth), we were ready to begin.

This time we worked backwards. Selecting stories from Judith Pasamanick's *Favorite Fables of Aesop*, I stated the moral *before* reading the tale aloud. What does this moral mean? I asked. Can you give examples of this meaning from your life? It wasn't until after the discussion that I read the fable aloud.

Here are some of their personal interpretations of the morals in the book.

MORAL: *Slow and steady wins the race.*

"One day I saw a drawing contest. So I joined in. When I got there, there were one girl and two boys. They were very good drawers. But slow and steady, I won the race." —Naiem

MORAL: *One good turn deserves another.*

"It means if you want someone to do something for you, you should do something for them. Once my mom had a lot of dishes to wash and my dad would not help her and my brother would not help her, And I would help her. And once I needed help with my room and my dad would not help me, my brother would not help me. But my mom would help me." —Casey

MORAL: *A liar will not be believed even when he tells the truth.*

"I think it means people will not believe something even when you tell the truth. When my brother was small, he said he was bigger than me. Maybe when he is bigger than me I won't believe him. I don't believe him even when he is smaller than me and he says he is bigger than me." —Patrick M.

Contemporary Authors Look Back

Do modern-day authors base their stories on fables and folktales from the past? To help children answer this, I introduced two works by the contemporary writer William Steig: *Amos and Boris* and *Dr. DeSoto*. Steig's stories—humorous, wise, and often award-winning—would entertain the class and, at the same time, help them answer this question.

I began with *Dr. DeSoto*, the story of a mouse dentist who outwits a fox. The fox plans to eat the mouse and his wife, but the rodents outsmart the fox in the end.

I gave my class a pre-listening assignment. "Listen to see which of Aesop's fables this story reminds you of," I said. Then I started reading. Before long, Krista exclaimed, "It's like 'The Wolf and the Crane'!" Mark concurred: "Both stories are about one animal helping another." Added Christina, "In both stories, the one who helped could have gotten hurt." Their comparisons were made quickly and excitedly.

"What are the differences in the stories?" I asked. Heather said, "In Aesop's story, the wolf wins. But in Steig's story, the fox, who is like the wolf, gets outsmarted." Casey added, "So the endings are different."

Noting Story Structure

The children also noticed that Steig's *Amos and Boris* and Aesop's "The Lion and the Mouse" contained strong thematic and plot similarities. Mark said, "The big animal helps the small animal. Then the big animal gets in trouble. And the small animal saves the big animal. I think it is the same moral."

Casey also noticed, "The two bigger animals don't expect anything bad to happen, but something bad did happen."

Naiem added, "They are the same by the way the smaller animals say they can't help them, but then they do help them."

Patrick remarked on this thematic difference: "In *Amos and Boris* the two animals are friends, but in Aesop's story they are not."

I was pleased with this discussion. The children saw that story lines from the past (such as those by Aesop) could be used as inspiration for stories of today (such as those by Steig, or by the children themselves). Children also recognized that similar tales could have different conclusions. I knew that this understanding would be helpful and empowering in our upcoming fairy tale unit. The children could look to the older fairy tales as models and as a source for ideas, but would realize that they could also change the messages conveyed.

Summing Up Thus Far (First Semester)

By studying the works of Dr. Seuss, Leo Lionni, and William Steig and the folklore attributed to Aesop, the children:

→ understood that books are written by people, and therefore, convey individual perspectives;

→ appreciated that authors often wish to convey these particular perspectives, messages, or morals through their stories;

→ understood that messages may be clearly stated or merely implied, perhaps leading to different interpretations by different readers/listeners;

➢ realized that the implied messages need to be inferred based on what the characters in the story did;

➢ noted that the reader/listener may agree or disagree with the author's message;

➢ understood that the writer may base his or her ideas on another storyteller or author's work but use those ideas in new ways; and

➢ found that a writer's work, while being faithful to an old form, can, in turn, be used to illuminate that writer's perspectives and/or messages.

Once my students were immersed in analyzing and interpreting specific literary works, according to plan, and were authors themselves, the above understandings were in place. The second half of the year would be spent applying these understandings to our study of fairy tales and their implied messages about gender roles.

CHAPTER 3

A Grimms' Fairy Tale Study

Introducing Writers from the Past

 At the start of the second half of our school year, I announced to my class that we would be studying the Grimm Brothers' fairy tales. I explained that the Grimms wrote down stories they had heard or read from folklore, but that they changed the stories in their own way. Jon raised his hand and said, "Then they probably had their own messages." A perceptive comment, I noted.

I asked the children: "What do you know about the Brothers Grimm?" Christina knew they lived a long time ago. Regina guessed they had good imaginations. Mark knew they were brothers but did not know how many brothers they were. I then offered specifics. (Much of my own research was based on work by Jack Zipes, primarily using *The Brothers Grimm*.) I shared the information with the class, then asked: "What information do you think would be important for us to write down about the Brothers Grimm?" In this way, I had them review the facts in their minds, reinforce their new knowledge, and develop reading skills as they read their dictated comments. They came up with the following list.

What Do We Know About the Brothers Grimm?

1. They were two brothers, Jacob and Wilhelm.

2. They lived in Germany.

3. They were born over 200 years ago.

4. They wrote stories based on folklore.

5. They invited storytellers to their homes and recorded their stories.

6. They learned other stories from books.

7. They wanted to find shared German culture through folklore.

8. They wrote the stories in their own way and changed them several times before publishing them.

9. The Grimms wanted to sell their stories.

10. The Grimms made some of the changes so parents would buy and read these stories to their children.

I asked the children, "What kind of changes do you think the Grimms might have made so parents would want to read these stories to children?"

Daniel: "Maybe they made them less scary."

Ayana: "Maybe they changed the messages."

Christina: "Maybe they changed the endings."

I told them that, in some cases, all their responses were true. I added, "Since the Grimms lived in Germany at a time when men were usually considered the 'bosses,' a writer of that time might want to show that in his or her stories. When we read the stories together, you might look for messages about how the writers thought men and women should behave."

Including a Critical Look at Gender Portrayals

After the discussion, I asked, "Do you have to agree with a writer's messages?" Mark, recalling our previous work on the subject, answered, "No. It's just that author's opinion."

"Do you think men's and women's roles and opportunities today are the same as they were in the Grimms' time in Germany?" I asked. "Remember, the Brothers Grimm were born over 200 years ago."

Andi said that she thought things were different today. "My mother might even become a judge."

Regina agreed that women could do more now than they could in the "olden days."

I said, "Let's remember this as we read the Grimms' fairy tales together and write down our observations."

Beginning with the Known

I began with fairy tales with which many children would be familiar. This would draw them in and ensure their comfort. Once they could establish certain regularities in the Grimms' fairy tale form and style, we would go on to less recognizable tales.

We began with *Little Red Cap*, or as the children knew it, *Little Red Riding Hood*. I said, "You know that fairy tales come from folklore, so there is no one correct way that the story goes. In fact, there can be many versions of the same tale. It all depends on who is telling or writing it. Before I read the Grimms' version of this story to you, I want you to share the story as you know it."

Many children in the class were eager to share this familiar story. Volunteers took turns telling it. Their version, down to Mark's unsolicited demonstration of the wagging of the mother's finger as she told Little Red Riding Hood not to stray from the path, was cautionary and moralistic. Shayna ended with, "And Little Red Riding Hood learned to listen to her mother and never, ever to stray from the path again."

I then read the Grimms' version of the tale to them. I said, "We will have time to share observations and comments when I am finished reading the story, so please hold your responses until then. For this first reading, let's listen carefully to the story and how it is told."

I could see sheer pleasure in many of the children's faces as they heard a familiar story that was written so well. At its completion, I asked, "How do you think this compares to the version you told?"

Anju: "The girl wore a little red cap instead of a cape with a hood. So she had a different name, too."

Casey: "There were more details, like about how the woods and people looked."

However, the class agreed that this story was similar to the one on which their version was based.

I asked, "How did the little girl save herself in this story?"

Christina: "She didn't. The hunter saved her."

"Could she have saved herself?" I inquired.

Christina thought for a few seconds. "She could have run away or fought the wolf off when she saw that it didn't really look like her grandmother in that bed."

A Writing Assignment

I learned that the Grimms also have a second version of *Little Red Cap*. This version is a sequel in which a wiser Little Red Cap and Grandma outwit the wolf. The women entice the wolf with the smell of cooked sausages. While seeking the source of the smell, the wolf falls down the chimney and into a trough of boiling water.

I read this version to the class and asked students which version they preferred and why. (I encourage my students to give their reasons. I feel this develops their ability to reason and to articulate their reasoning. What's more, they are drawn away from simplistic answers.)

The majority of the class wrote that they preferred the outcome of the second, less familiar story. For example: "I liked the last version we read because Little Red Cap was smarter by not being disturbed by the wolf and going straight to Grandma's house. And the Grandma was really smart this time. This time Grandma and Little Red Cap helped each other get away so they wouldn't get eaten by the wolf."—Anju

Anju was able to grasp two important themes in this second version—the importance of teamwork and the ability to use one's wits to escape from a dangerous situation. I was excited to see that the children could appreciate these qualities in the female characters. These students had developed a different mind-set, as had I, than the class with which I began my fairy tale studies. Our discussions and earlier work on critical thinking must have made a difference.

Another Comparison

The next story we studied was *Cinderella*. Before reading it aloud, I asked children to retell the story as they knew it. For the most part, children remembered the animated movie version of the tale. I decided to use this familiarity with the Disney version as a learning experience. How were the characters depicted? What values did they convey? We would soon talk this over.

I saw this as a teachable moment. I could reemphasize that folktales are continually being changed, depending on the teller, the audience, the purpose for the telling, and the time and place. Therefore, we backtracked to review the animated film version to see how it departed from the Grimms' literary versions. If it departed greatly, what might be the reason?

So we watched and critiqued the animated film versions of the popular tales *Cinderella, Snow White and the Seven Dwarfs*, and *Sleeping Beauty* after hearing the Grimms' versions. We compared and contrasted the movies with the Grimms' versions. One of my aims was to show children that, in their later writing, they too could alter the fairy tales they knew to depict their own views of people and their roles for their own purposes.

Clarifying Structure and Commonalities in the Grimms' Tales

Snow White, Rumplestiltskin, and *Hansel and Gretel* were the next tales I read aloud. "What did you think of the story?" I asked after reading each aloud. "How is this story similar to other Grimms stories that I've read to you?"

I jotted down their observations on chart paper and added to the chart each day. We were creating an expanding list available to read, reread, and study on a continuous basis. Each child also wrote personal responses to the stories in his or her notebook.

To clarify the story structure, I created another chart. Children contributed ideas after a second reading of each tale. That chart can be found on pages 30 and 31.

STORY STRUCTURE CHART

TITLE	CHARACTERS	PROBLEMS
Cinderella	Cinderella; birds over mother's grave; stepmother; 2 stepsisters; prince; father; real mother;	Cinderella's mother dies and she is treated very poorly by stepmother and stepsisters.
Snow White	Snow White; real mother; stepmother; father; 7 dwarves; prince	Stepmother orders Snow White killed because she is jealous of Snow White's beauty.
Rumplestiltskin	Rumplestiltskin; miller's daughter; miller; king; king's messenger	King wants miller's daughter to spin straw into gold. She cannot do it.
Hansel and Gretel	Hansel; Gretel; stepmother; father; various birds	1. Children left in woods to be eaten or to starve. 2. The witch plans to eat them.
Little Red Cap	Little Red Cap; mother; wolf; grandmother; hunter	Wolf eats grandmother and Little Red Cap.
The Frog Prince	princess; frog; king	1. Princess drops ball into well. 2. Princess does not want to keep promise to frog.
Rapunzel	Rapunzel; sorceress; mother; father; prince	1. Mother will only eat the Rapunzel lettuce of sorceress. 2. Rapunzel locked in tower by sorceress.
Briar Rose	Briar Rose; king; queen; 3 wise women; prince	1. King and queen cannot have child. 2. 13th wise woman casts spell on kingdom.
The White Snake	servant; first and second king; birds; fish; ants; horse; ducks; princess	1. Queen loses ring. Servant is accused. 2. Servant wants to marry princess but must do tasks.
The Juniper Tree	boy; sister; father; real mother; stepmother; goldsmith; shoemaker; millers	1. Mother dies. Stepmother kills boy. 2. Boy turns into a bird.

SOLUTIONS	RESOLUTION
The birds from mother's grave helped her meet the prince.	Cinderella marries the prince. Sisters are blinded by birds.
Wild boar is killed instead of Snow White. Snow White stays with dwarves until stepmother puts her to death by feeding her a poisoned apple.	Unconscious Snow White given to prince. Coffin drops and apple falls out. Snow White is alive and marries prince. Stepmother dies, dancing in burning shoes.
Rumplestiltskin helps, but by the third time asks for first-born child as payment, unless she can guess his name.	Messenger discovers Rumplestiltskin's name. Miller's daughter keeps child as bargained. Rumplestiltskin tears himself in half.
Children leave pebbles to find way home. When kept by witch, Gretel shuts oven door on her.	Children come home. Father is happy to see them. Stepmother is dead. Children bring jewels home.
Hunter cuts wolf open. He rescues Little Red Cap and grandmother.	Wolf's stomach is filled with rocks and he dies. Hunter takes the wolf's fur home. Grandma and Little Red Cap have wine and cake.
1. Frog gets ball on condition of being princess's companion. 2. Father makes princess keep her promise to the frog.	Princess throws frog against the wall. He turns into a prince.
1. Rapunzel lettuce given in exchange for child. 2. Rapunzel lets her hair down for prince to climb up.	Prince gets blinded by thorns but is reunited with Rapunzel and gets back his eyesight.
1. Frog grants wish. 2. 100 years go by. Spell is broken.	Everyone wakes up. Prince marries Briar Rose.
1. Servant eats white snake and can communicate with animals. 2. Animals help with tasks.	Servant marries princess.
1. Stepmother makes it look like sister killed boy. 2. Bird reveals story in song.	Bird drops stone on stepmother. Boy is transformed back into himself.

Student-Raised Issues

Sometimes children brought up specific issues and we focused on those issues in the class discussion. For example, after hearing *Rumplestiltskin*, Krista said, "I think the father was wrong to lie to the king." Seymour said, "I think the king was greedy."

I asked the children to write about who they thought was the worst villain in the story. Again, I added, "Be sure, as always, to write why you believe what you do." Here are samples of their writing on this topic.

> "I think the real villain is the father because he gets his daughter in danger by going to the king to show off and saying, 'My daughter can do this and that.' He said it to the king and the king put the daughter in a room and almost killed her."
> —Krista

> "I think the villain was the king because the king did not love her. The king wanted her for the gold. The king made her make gold for three days. The king said, 'If you don't do it you die.' Not only did the king not love her but the king would kill her."
> —Daniel

> "I think the villain is the father because he started everything and he bragged that she could spin straw into gold and that made her almost killed. And made her lose her precious things. And made her baby almost gone. And made her guess all those names. And made the messenger go over a mountain. And made Rumplestiltskin sad. And made Rumplestiltskin die."
> —Naiem

It was clear to me that my students were not merely accepting the patriarchal order of things as put forth in this story. They were aware of, and sensitive to, the inhumanity in the way the king and father were using their powers over the girl.

Seeking Alternative Solutions

One day, after reading the story *The Frog Prince*, Andi said, "The princess didn't even try to get the ball back. She just cried."

I saw this as an excellent opportunity to encourage the children to find alternative and more active solutions for the female characters. So I told the class: "Write what you could have done if you were the princess who lost your ball down the well."

Initially, some children were at a loss. I allowed and, in some cases, initiated small-group discussions so they could react to one anothers' ideas. This worked well. No sooner had one child made a statement than others responded to it, or filled in details.

Patrick and Casey asked to share their written solutions with the class. You can see how one version built on the other:

> "If I were the princess, I would get a net and a ladder and go down the ladder and catch it with the net and go back up again."
> —Patrick M.

> "If I were the princess, I would go tell my father that my ball fell into the well. Then I would go get a net from the storage closet and get my ball. Then I would not play with my ball by the well anymore. Or I would ask my father if I could smash my crown and make another ball."
> —Casey

It was a delight for me to witness the students' ability to visualize and articulate a more active role for the female in this story. I looked forward to continuing the "If I were..." exercises.

Rapunzel and *Briar Rose* were the last two of the already familiar Grimms stories that I read to the class. Briar Rose is more popularly known as *Sleeping Beauty*.

With Rapunzel, my class again sought more active alternatives for the heroine by using the "If I were..." exercise and small-group discussion. Here are examples of their writing.

> "If I were Rapunzel, I would cut off my hair and attach it to the hook and climb down it myself."   —Andi

> "If I were Rapunzel, I would climb down by the stones and run real fast and then cut my hair up to my waist and get rid of it."   —Anju

The day after we shared these responses, I asked the class to work in small groups to discuss who their favorite character in this story was. I again reminded them of the need to justify their opinions—to tell why. I said, "Before you choose your favorite character, review what the characters in the story do and why. For example, you might think about why the witch wanted to keep Rapunzel in the tower."

Anju took my advice and clearly looked at motivation. She wrote: "My favorite character was the witch because she was very lonely and didn't want to lose a child. Boy, was she lonely. And she didn't want the prince to take Rapunzel. The witch wanted to keep her so that she wasn't that lonely. And she was kind of nice in a way.

This is how she was kind: She didn't want to hurt Rapunzel. She just wanted to keep her."

> "My favorite character is Rapunzel because it's funny when she says, 'You're much heavier than the prince.' It's funny that she's so stupid."
> —Andi

I think Andi's reaction was a direct result of the exercises we had been doing in class. I had asked them to put themselves in the place of the heroine and find more active and beneficial solutions to given problems in the stories. Andi found an incongruence between an intelligent response on the part of Rapunzel and the one given in the story. It was wonderful to me that Andi was not blindly accepting the lack of thought evidenced by the heroine. Instead she was reacting and responding with independence of her own.

Looking at Less Familiar Tales

We were now ready to examine stories that would probably be new to the children. This would be the class's first encounter with two powerful stories in the Grimms' collection—*The White Snake* and *The Juniper Tree*. Now that students knew the structure and general outcome of the Grimms' tales, I thought they would be able to accept what might otherwise have been frightening events in these stories.

The White Snake is about a trusted servant who acquires the ability to understand the language of animals when he tastes a white snake. He is sentenced to be executed by the king. *The Juniper Tree* is about a wicked stepmother. Though she closes a lid on her stepson's head, he comes back to life with the help of a magic bird.

Students were engrossed but *not* frightened while they listened to these stories. Instead, they predicted happy endings for the characters in question. After I read *The Juniper Tree*, I asked them what it reminded them of. The class quickly made connections to other Grimms' tales, connecting the new to the known.

> "This story made me think of *Rumplestiltskin* because every time one of the men asked the bird to sing, the bird told the men to give up something. The part I like is when the boy came back alive. And the part I didn't like is when the wife cut off the boy's head. And another reason I like the story is because the boy's sister wasn't evil like his mother." —Shayna

> "It reminds me of *Hansel and Gretel* because when Gretel closed the lid..."
> —Jon

"I thought it was weird because it is very weird when a person eats someone else. It reminded me of *Rumplestiltskin* because the bird would ask for something. It reminded me of *Snow White* because the boy's mother said, 'Oh how I wish for a child as white as snow and black.' It reminded me of *Cinderella* because the girl's mom is mean and Cinderella's mom is mean. I liked the part when the mother gets hit on the head with a rock because she deserved it because she was cruel, mean, selfish, unkind and also she chopped the boy's head off so that's why she really deserved it."

—Anju

Interestingly, Patrick M. was reminded of an Aesop fable, drawing on our first semester:

"It reminded me of *The Lion and the Mouse* because the people did something to the bird and the bird did something to the people."

—Patrick

Analyzing the Grimms' Fairy Tales: Strategies That Worked

1. Often, children were already familiar with a fairy tale, or a version of it, before I read it in class. In that case, I asked volunteers to tell their version aloud. Then I read the Grimms' version to the class.

2. We compared the children's versions with each other, and with the tale I read aloud. Children responded to the tales as a whole class or in small groups.

3. I wrote their comments on chart paper (see sample, What Have We Learned About Grimms' Fairy Tales?, page 36).

4. Children responded in writing.

5. On another day, the class focused on the story's structure. Children dictated comments as I wrote on the Story Structure Chart.

6. Now that the children were clear about the story's structure, and could retell the story based on this knowledge, they were able to act it out. I read the story a second time, while children performed for each other.

What Have We Learned About the Grimms' Fairy Tales?

1. The numbers 3, 7, 12, and 100 are special.
2. The older women are often mean and/or ugly.
3. The men are often brave but not smart.
4. The good people have good endings.
5. The bad people get punished.
6. The good mothers die when their children are born.
7. The fathers then marry bad mothers.
8. The girls cry when they are in trouble.
9. The fathers do not help their children.
10. There is a lot of violence.
11. People sometimes eat other people.
12. Dead people can come back to life.
13. Spells are cast.
14. There is fighting and blood.
15. The stories happened a long time ago.
16. Characters are usually princes, princesses, kings, queens, servants, and witches.
17. The middle part is scary.
18. Men go only for beauty.
19. Often there are repeating chants.
20. People are given tasks.
21. Princesses are always pretty.
22. Animals are helpers.
23. Princesses do not think for themselves.
24. There is magic in the story.
25. Somebody usually dies.
26. Characters trade favors.
27. A character is often lonely and wants a baby.
28. Women need to be saved.
29. Stepparents do not help their stepchildren.
30. Dead people are often buried under trees.
31. Stepparents are mothers, not fathers.
32. Only boys go into the woods to seek their fortunes.
33. Usually, beauty on the outside means being good inside.
34. Usually the mean people are ugly.
35. Stepmothers have their own daughters but not their own sons.
36. Flowers are used to show things coming back to life.
37. Boys speak up more.
38. Only the girls do the housework.
39. There are magical helpers.

Conclusion

I was pleased that my students not only enjoyed the fairy tales, but that they had also obviously attained a high level of fairy tale scholarship. They relished the sounds of the stories and were captivated by the story elements, from enchanted castles to magical helpers. The more stories they heard, the richer their foundation for how stories sound and develop.

Then, too, children realized that characters in Grimms' tales were portrayed in distinctive ways. Children learned to generalize about those characters, both within a story and between stories. For example, they learned that in Grimms' tales, women were often portrayed as weak or helpless and men were portrayed as saviors.

Using the dynamics of group discussion and interaction, which I moderated, as well as thoughtful listening, questioning, and reflection on all our parts, children were developing the ability to react perceptively to the stories and to the writers, to discern implied messages about gender roles in the tales, and to become critical thinkers by habit.

Chapter 4

Comparing Gender Roles in Grimms' Tales with Alternative Models

Children Respond to Our Chart

 One day I reviewed the chart children had dictated earlier about Grimms' fairytales (see page 41). This time I focused on how observant children were becoming about gender issues raised in these stories. I discovered that, of the 39 observations the current class dictated, 17 (almost half of the total) dealt directly with that issue. I was pleased that children were becoming increasingly aware.

To examine this further, I asked, "How do you feel about the ways in which men and women are pictured in these fairy tales?"

> "I don't think it's always like that. Women can be brave, too. And boys cry, too."
> —Christina

> "Just because grandmothers are old doesn't mean they get mean."
> —Danny

> "Boys don't have to speak more. I like to speak in class."
> —Andi

Jon talked about how he and his father do art together, and Marley spoke about reading together with his father. Patrick talked about how his grandmother took care of him while his mother worked, and Casey talked about how she loved her grandmother.

In many ways, my students spoke about how their own experiences refuted the stereotypical messages in these stories. In this way, they were able to talk about the depiction of men and women and to think on a high level about the material.

Introduction to "Modern" Fairy Tales

I told my students that they were not the only people who have taken issue with gender depictions in these tales. At this time, I introduced my students to some modern authors who have written fairy tales that reflect less rigid role models for men and women, in part, in response to the traditional tales.

I brought to class *Don't Bet on the Prince: Contemporary Feminist Fairy Tales in North America and England* by Jack Zipes. This book is divided into three parts: Feminist Fairy Tales for Young (and Old) Readers, Feminist Fairy Tales for Old (and Young) Readers, and Feminist Literary Criticism. I read aloud stories from Section

One. (Each of these stories, in some way, challenges at least one of the gender stereotypes the children noted in the traditional tales.)

I also read *Sleeping Ugly* by Jane Yolen, a tale in which beauty and goodness are no longer equated.

What Have We Learned About the Grimms' Fairy Tales?

1. The numbers 3, 7, 12, and 100 are special.
2. The older women are often mean and/or ugly.
3. The men are often brave but not smart.
4. The good people have good endings.
5. The bad people get punished.
6. The good mothers die when their children are born.
7. The fathers then marry bad mothers.
8. The girls cry when they are in trouble.
9. The fathers do not help their children.
10. There is a lot of violence.
11. People sometimes eat other people.
12. Dead people can come back to life.
13. Spells are cast.
14. There is fighting and blood.
15. The stories happened a long time ago.
16. Characters are usually princes, princesses, kings, queens, servants, and witches.
17. The middle part is scary.
18. Men go only for beauty.
19. Often there are repeating chants.
20. People are given tasks.
21. Princesses are always pretty.
22. Animals are helpers.
23. Princesses do not think for themselves.
24. There is magic in the story.
25. Somebody usually dies.
26. Characters trade favors.
27. A character is often lonely and wants a baby.
28. Women need to be saved.
29. Stepparents do not help their stepchildren.
30. Dead people are often buried under trees.
31. Stepparents are mothers, not fathers.
32. Only boys go into the woods to seek their fortunes.
33. Usually, beauty on the outside means being good inside.
34. Usually the mean people are ugly.
35. Stepmothers have their own daughters but not their own sons.
36. Flowers are used to show things coming back to life.
37. Boys speak up more.
38. Only the girls do the housework.
39. There are magical helpers.

Pre-Writing Techniques

I asked students to listen carefully to these tales. I also told them, "Begin to think about designing your own stories that will show your own thoughts about how men and women can behave, just as these authors have done."

I structured the unit in the same way I had with the Grimms' work: I read each story aloud twice, on separate days. After the first reading, the children discussed their responses as a whole class or in small groups. Before the second reading, the children dictated the elements of the story structure that they noticed and I wrote on the story structure chart (see pages 44 and 45). During the second reading, they enacted the tale while I narrated. Although I read the story verbatim, children had the freedom to add dialogue during their enactments as they saw fit.

Changes in Approach

During the reading of these stories, students' responses were now highly focused on the less rigid gender roles. Despite these changes from the Grimms, the children could see from the story structure chart that these were still indeed fairy tales. I now felt that students might be able to write fairy tales of their own. For their original stories, I wanted them to think of ways in which gender roles, as characterized by the Grimms, could be changed. I asked children to suggest strategies writers can use, many of which they saw modeled in the modern stories I read to them. I recorded their ideas on a chart (see page 43).

I believe this lesson freed children to think more flexibly about characters' roles and behavior. I recognized, of course, that children also need to feel free to cast characters in traditional roles, if they so choose.

A Look at Some Retold Multicultural Folklore

I then introduced *Tatterhood and Other Tales*, edited by Ethel Johnston Phelps. This book is an anthology of retold tales from multicultural folklore. The focus in each of these fairly recent retellings is on an active and resourceful heroine. I read the following stories from this volume.

1. *Tatterhood*, based on a Norwegian folktale. This is a story about two

How can modern writers change the way men and women are shown in the Grimms' fairy tales?

1. Boys and girls can learn to make their own decisions.
2. Girls do not have to marry princes.
3. Boys do not have to marry princesses.
4. Both women and men can stand up for themselves.
5. The girls can be good at math.
6. All people can learn to listen to themselves.
7. Witches can be nice.
8. Not all princes have to be brave.
9. Girls can also seek their fortunes.
10. People can be good-looking outside but mean inside.
11. Girls and boys can decide not to marry.
12. Older women can be helpful and kind, and not jealous.
13. Men can do housework, too.
14. You don't have to be beautiful outside to be good inside.
15. Who you are is more important than how you look.
16. Both girls and boys can rescue others.
17. Boys can be rescued.
18. Girls can be brave.
19. Both boys and girls can save themselves and others by thinking.
20. Boys can like to read and do quiet activities.
21. You can change things by understanding others instead of fighting them.
22. Men can be gentle.
23. Men and women can cooperate and work together.
24. Girls can be confident.
25. People can choose to do work helping others instead of becoming princes or princesses.
26. People can prefer freedom to being rich.
27. Girls can keep trying to get what they want instead of just crying.

sisters. One sister, Tatterhood, is unconventional, capable, and independent. After many adventures, she saves her sister and meets a prince who enjoys and respects her individuality.

2. *Unanana and the Elephant,* based on a tale from southern Africa. In this story, a brave and clever mother rescues her children (and many others) from the belly of an elephant.

3. *The Hedley Kow,* from the Sudanese region of the Nile River. The heroine

STORY STRUCTURE CHART: MODERN FAIRY TALES

TITLE AND AUTHOR	CHARACTERS	PROBLEMS
The Princess Who Stood on Her Own Two Feet by Jeanne Desy	Princess; dog/prince; prince; wizard; parents; cat	The princess wants to marry the prince but he thinks she is too tall, too smart, and he doesn't like her dog.
Prince Amilec by Tanith Lee	Prince Amilec; witch princess; Basil the bat; king and queen; wizard; messenger	1. Princess does not want to marry but her parents want her to marry. 2. Princess gives Prince Amilec three difficult tasks.
Sleeping Ugly by Jane Yolen	Plain Jane; Princess Miserella; Prince Jojo; fairy	1. Princess Miserella could not find her way home. 2. The fairy has them all fall asleep for 100 years.
Petronella by Jay Williams	2 brothers; Petronella; little old man; Wizard Albion; Prince Ferdinand	1. Petronella wants to seek her fortune but she is told not to because she is a girl. 2. Petronella wants to rescue the prince and is given three tasks. 3. The prince does not want to be rescued.
The Donkey Prince by Angela Carter	Daisy; queen; queen's father; donkey (Bruno); Wildman Terror	1. The queen did not give the apple to the donkey. Then she finds out that the apple would have removed the donkey's spell. 2. The queen's apple is taken.
Russalka or the Seacoast of Bohemia by Joanna Russ	Russalka; prince; sea witch; wizard	1. Russalka wants to be human and marry a prince. 2. Russalka and the prince are not happy together.
Snow White by Merseyside Story Collective	Snow White; 7 dwarfs; Magic Mirror; queen; soldiers	The people do all the work, but the queen gets everything. The people are poor.
The Moon Ribbon by Jane Yolen	Silva; real mother; stepmother; father; stepsisters	Stepmother and stepsisters are mean to Silva.

SOLUTIONS	RESOLUTION
1. The princess pretends she cannot walk or talk. **2.** The dog dies because he loves her.	The dog comes back to life as a prince. He likes and loves the princess as she is.
The beautiful witch uses magic to help Prince Amilec accomplish his tasks.	Prince Amilec decides to marry the witch instead. The princess travels and meets a prince that acts like she does. She is given a task. She seeks a wizard for help.
1. The Good Fairy takes her to Plain Jane's house. **2.** The prince kisses the Good Fairy and Plain Jane and they wake up.	Prince Jojo marries Plain Jane. Princess Miserella stays asleep.
1. She insists on going. **2.** She understands and helps the animals instead of weeping or fighting to accomplish her tasks.	Petronella marries the wizard instead.
1. She takes the donkey and raises him as a prince so a man and woman will go through fire and water for him. **2.** Donkey and Daisy go to the mountain to get the apple.	Apple is retrieved. Daisy and Wildman go through fire and water. Donkeys turn back to men. Daisy and Bruno get married.
1. Russalka goes to the sea witch and is transformed into an almost human girl. **2.** Prince asks wizards to help her become more humanlike.	The sea witch's spell is removed by a wizard. Russalka turns back into a mermaid and dies out of the water.
Snow White organizes the people to fight against the queen.	The queen tries to throw the mirror at the people and she falls with it.
Stepmother and stepsisters go underground by following the ribbon.	Silva gives the silver ribbon to her own daughter who then gives it to her daughter. She lives happily and now owns her house.

of this story is a fearless older woman who good-naturedly befriends the village bogie.

4. *Janet and Tamlin*, from Scotland. Janet bravely saves her lover from the enchantment of the Queen of Elfland.

5. *What Happened to Six Wives Who Ate Onions*, a Native American tale. In this story, the wives join together and seek a separate existence in the sky, rather than submitting to their husbands' wishes.

6. *Kate Crackernuts*, from the Orkney Islands off Scotland. Kate, the heroine, saves both her sister and a prince from their enchantments.

7. *Three Strong Women*, from Japan. By working with a young woman named Maru-me, her mother, and her grandmother, a famous wrestler learns to be stronger. He and Maru-me also enter an egalitarian marriage.

8. *The Black Bull of Norroway*, from England. In this story, the heroine successfully performs demanding tasks to free her loved one, the Black Bull, from the trolls' spell.

After hearing the stories, we added to our chart the following possible character traits and actions for men and women in fairy tales.

---

28. Some men like poetry better than fighting.
29. Some women are stronger than some men.
30. <u>We all have different kinds of strength</u>.
31. Older people are not always weak.
32. Problems can be solved without fighting.
33. People should not accept being treated badly.
34. Men and women can help each other.

Defining True Strength

I especially wanted my students to examine number 30—We all have different kinds of strength—because in these alternative fairy tales, women, in various ways, were in control of their own lives. However, unlike the heroes in more traditional tales, physical strength and bravery in battle were not necessarily the key to winning. Children began to develop a more multifaceted perspective as to what strength could be. They began to incorporate some traditional "female" traits, like compassion, caring, empathy, and the ability to maintain composure under stress, into their definitions of strength for both men and women.

In that context, I asked the students to write about what it was that they considered to be true strength and to give an example from their lives.

WHAT IS TRUE STRENGTH?

I believe true strength is love—the kind of love that gives care and comfort is one kind of love. Another kind of strength is to stand up to your own problems. Another kind of strength is to go by your beliefs. All of these strengths come from your brain. My grandpa is showing strength by helping my grandma.

—Heather B.

Name: Heather
Date: 1/4

In some modern fairy tales we have been reading, true strength does not always mean having strong muscles. What do you think true strength is? Why? Give an example.

I belive that true strength is Love. The kind of love that give care and comfort is one tipe of strength. Another Kind of strength is to stand up to your own problems. Another Kind of strength is to go by your beliefs. All of these strengths come from your brain. My grampa is showing strength by helping my grandma.

Name: Khalia
Date: January 5

In some modern fairy tales we have been reading, true strength does not always mean having strong muscles. What do you think true strength is? Why? Give an example.

If your friend had tried drug's and they ask you to try it and you new it was bad and you sed no. True strength is saying no to somthing that you no is wrong.

If your friend had tried drugs and they ask you to try it and you knew it was bad and you said no. True strength is saying no to something you know is wrong.

—Khalia

47

An example of true strength is like a kid being beat up and another kid said stop and warned that he would tell.

—Daniel

Being kind because you can do important things like feed the homeless. Once me and my mom saw a homeless person and we fed him.

—Alexandra

The children were not only looking at and critiquing gender roles in fairy tales, they were also applying these critiques to real-life situations. They were also becoming increasingly aware that writers, in their own stories, could change limitations based on gender in ways they saw fit. It was exhilarating to see the development of my students' thinking. The next step was for them to become writers of fairy tales themselves!

CHAPTER 5

The Children Write Original Fairy Tales

Getting Started

✤ I was confident that my students had internalized the structure of fairy tales. I felt they were ready to write fairy tales of their own.

I looked back at original stories created by former students over the last two years. In those cases, I had asked students to create outlines before writing. Perhaps the rigid adherence to their outlines might have stilted their writing, I thought. I decided to allow my present students to write freely, and to help them check on structural elements after the drafts were penned.

During writing workshop, I moved around the room, conferring with individual children as needed. I told them that, for now, the stories they were writing were drafts. At a later time, they could choose their favorite piece to develop and publish.

What Worked

If children had trouble getting started, I gave them the following possible options.

1. Write your own version of a story you know. You can change any part of the story.

2. Write a new ending for a known fairy tale.

3. Write a sequel to one of the stories.

4. Change a story by putting yourself or somebody else in place of one of the characters.

5. Change the time and location in which the story takes place.

6. Think of a new problem that the characters must solve.

Posing Helpful Questions

✤ As I walked around the room, I read what the children had written and asked questions helping them clarify detail and/or structure. Through small, impromptu mini-conferences I was able to nudge children to find solutions to the obstacles they were encountering.

Here are some examples of my exchanges with students.

➜ Heather noticed that the characters in her story seemed flat. "Can you write down *exactly* what the characters said, rather than describing their conversation?" I commented. Heather then created the following dialogue:

> But she just ignored him and said, "You think I am going home with you? Well—no way!"
>
> "Well," he said, "now that is an order," as he grabbed her arm.

→ Anju had a fine opening line: "Once there was a princess who loved nature." Her story then continued. I asked her, "How can you show the reader that the princess loved nature?" Anju added, "She had plants all over the house and she had a greenhouse." Anju learned to show, not just tell.

→ I asked Daniel L. which "she" in his story was Little Red Cap and which "she" was Grandma. He realized that he needed to state the characters by name more often.

→ Seymour's story, I felt, needed closure. I asked him, "How does the story end?" He then added, "Then he just enjoys himself." This created a more satisfying ending.

In this way, the questions helped improve the students' writing.

Selecting a Story for Presentation

I was impressed with the originality of the children's work and how personal each story was. After a few weeks, I said, "I want you to think about which of the stories you have written you would most like to make into an illustrated book." It was only after they had chosen their stories that I asked the students to analyze them for structure by using the following sheet.

Name _____ Date_____

We have read Grimms' fairy tales and modern reworkings.
We are currently reading new fairy tales in which female heroines actively solve problems, and both men and women choose how they would like to lead their lives.
Begin to design your own fairy tale (or you may have already started) by answering the following questions. Remember the special characters, places, magic, and numbers used in fairy tales.

1. When and where does your tale take place?

_____

_____

2. Who are your characters?

_____

_____

3. What is the problem?

_____

_____

4. How do the heroes/heroines solve the problem?

_____

_____

5. What happens in the end?

_____

_____

In some cases, children read the sheet and compared it with their works in progress. They noticed that some parts of their stories were missing (a good opening line, an ending). They went back to their stories and revised. In some cases, the section was only one sentence, but it improved the piece nevertheless.

Name _Andi_   Date _May 26_

We have read Grimms' fairy tales and modern reworkings.
We are currently reading new fairy tales in which female heroines actively solve problems and both men and women choose how they would like to lead their lives.
Begin to design your own fairy tale (or you may have already started) by answering the following questions. Remember the special characters, places, magic, and numbers used in fairy tales.

1. When and where does your tale take place?
   a long time ago in a house.

2. Who are your characters?
   real mother and father, girl, step parents

3. What is the problem?
   1. girls mother and father die 2. step father is mean

4. How do the heroes/heroines solve the problem?
   1. girl finds step parents 2. she hers a voice and goes in magic door.

5. What happens in the end?
   father is nice for the rest of his life

Name _Anju_   Date _May 26_

We have read Grimms' fairy tales and modern reworkings.
We are currently reading new fairy tales in which female heroines actively solve problems and both men and women choose how they would like to lead their lives.
Begin to design your own fairy tale (or you may have already started) by answering the following questions. Remember the special characters, places, magic, and numbers used in fairy tales.

1. When and where does your tale take place?
   My story takes place in a house

2. Who are your characters?
   A bad prince, A good prince, cat, princess

3. What is the problem?
   The prince doesn't like cats.

4. How do the heroes/heroines solve the problem?
   The princess stopped the prince

5. What happens in the end?
   The princess marrys a better prince

Revising and Editing

Once children chose the fairy tale they wanted to publish, they read their drafts to me. Some children had drafts of several stories from which to choose. Generally I supported their decisions, although I sometimes asked children to show me other drafts, to be sure they'd thought through their decisions and hadn't merely picked a story at random.

For example, when I asked Andi why she chose *The Magic Door* over several other fine stories, she responded, "I like the way the door opens up and so does the father—he becomes nice." I could see her point.

I then went over the children's writing to discuss the content and structure of their chosen tales. They added clarifying details which emerged from our conferences.

The next step was for the children to edit the stories, and to check with me regarding spelling, capitalization, and punctuation.

Making Actual Books

Using blank books, the children now rewrote their stories, adding an illustration on each page. Depending on the length of their stories, they wrote one or more sentences on a page.

I asked them to prepare their initial illustrations in pencil so that they could erase (modify) them at a later time, if needed. When children were satisfied with their work, they colored their drawings with markers. They also wrote summaries of their stories on the back of the book (blurbs) and included authors' profiles on the inside covers. I showed them examples of front and back matter from the books we had in the classroom.

What struck me most about their stories was that, while each child did not attempt to use all our observations about gender issues in his or her story, each one did incorporate at least one of the gender issues we had discussed. And that seemed to be the very issue that struck each individual child most profoundly. I was often touched by their tales. I felt that these authors would move mountains! On the following pages you will find some samples of the childrens' fairy tales, along with my comments.

The Princess That Cared Only About Nature by Anju

In Anju's story, a prince is not allowed to come between a princess and the pet she loved. Refusing to be wed to the prince, the heroine sticks up for what she wants. Anju did use the fairy tale tradition of severe punishments; however, the object of punishment differed. Unlike in the Grimms tales, there can be a mean prince. Youth and beauty are not necessarily equated with goodness in this tale.

The Magical Princess by Christina

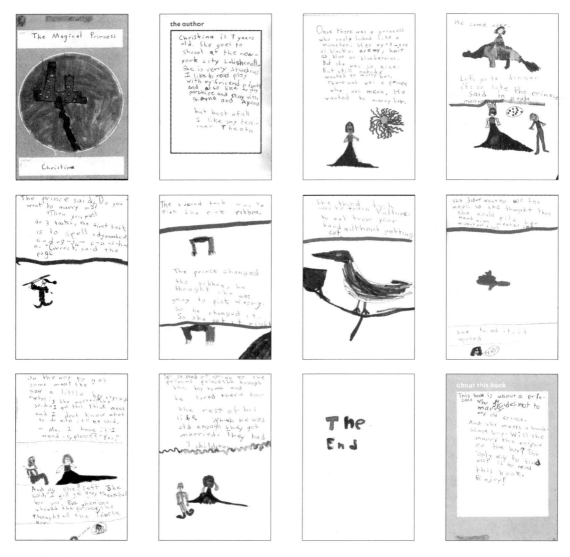

Christina jumps right in to contradict the idea that inner and outer beauty need be equated. Then, using humor, excellent detail, and dialogue, she reverses the gender roles in declaring who must do the three tasks. In this case, the jobs fall to the princess. I loved Christina's ending. While in traditional fairy tales marriage is used as a means of attaining wealth or higher class standing for women, this is not the case here. In Christina's tale, the princess chooses to marry a kind, rather than rich, boy.

Also of interest: Christina switches the traditional age relationship for this couple—the princess is older than her husband.

The Magic Door by Andi

Notice that Andi used an element that appears in many fairy tales: The couple wants a baby but must pay a price to have this wish fulfilled. Ani changed the traditional consequence, though, so that not only does the real mother die, but the real father dies as well. The girl then finds new parents. In Grimms tales the stepmother is often mean. In Andi's tale, however, the stepmother is kind and it is the stepfather who makes the girl do all the work.

In addition, a transformation takes place through magic. However, the transformation is nontraditional—the stepfather changes by becoming a better parent.

A Wizard Meets a Wizard by Patrick M.

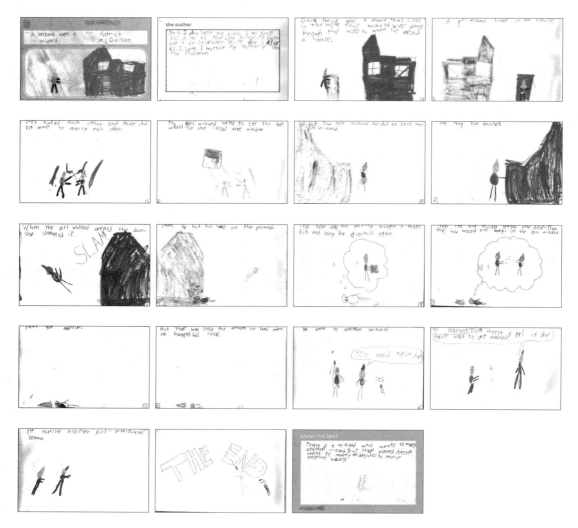

This author modeled many traditional tales in that a character goes through the woods. Patrick also included magic, but he played with it. Here, the magic only achieved the boy wizard's aim in his dream. In this case, the wizard merely imparted some real wisdom—"Don't marry a girl if she doesn't want to get married." There is hope for a marriage of equity here, for the boy wizard did not marry a girl who needed to be saved, but married another wizard, instead.

There's That Prince by Heather

The setting of this tale includes a prince who lives in a castle in the woods. The author then turns this into an alternative tale. Heather depicts, in wonderful dialogue and with outstanding drawings, a princess who uses her wits. Her princess is not coerced.

Little Red Cap by Daniel

I love this new version of Little Red Cap. *Daniel played beautifully with the material, including an idea to dress up as the* Three Little Pigs *and Arnold Lobel's* Frog and Toad *in order to outwit the fox of the story. The resourceful females in this tale finally come upon a successful plan. They team up to masquerade as cops and bring the fox to jail. (No naive and helpless girls here!) And the females, instead of competing against each other, join forces toward a common end.*

General Comments

Looking back at the stories, I am amazed at, and happy with, the achievement of my first and second graders. The work shows that the children not only grew in their ability to tell gripping tales with sound structures, but also understood ways to play with the content while remaining true to the form of fairy tale.

As can be seen from their work, there was, naturally, a wide range in the children's developmental writing abilities. However, during the process leading up to, and in the writing of these stories, the children also focused on issues important to society. While developing their critical thinking abilities, children maintained their wonderful childlike outlooks, styles, and joy. This, too, is apparent in their stories. Their optimism and sense of fairness was, and is, an inspiration to me.

Class Celebration

As each child completed his or her illustrated fairy tale, he or she became our celebrated author of the day. That youngster read the tale to the class, fielded questions and comments, and chose a part to play as the story was enacted by class members. Their satisfaction seemed as great as mine.

Jon pens his final version.

Children work on their original fairy tales.

Andi and Mark confer.

Children work on their illustrations.

Krista proudly shares her finished tale.

Andi reads from her book.

Heather, Ayana, and Vivian display their covers.

Casey and Anju are proud authors!

Andi shows how the door opens in her story.

CHAPTER 6

Fairy Tales Across the Curriculum

The activities described in the previous chapters took place daily and formed the core of the unit. I also integrated the fairy tales into other parts of the curriculum. Here are some examples.

Language Arts

In addition to the activities mentioned throughout this book, children also:

➔read published fairy tales silently in class,

➔read the charts to which they had contributed,

➔read the fairy tales I had previously read to them, and

➔read each other's original stories.

The reading I had done aloud now served as a model for children's own reading.

ILLUSTRATING THEIR WORK

I invited the children to illustrate the pages of their original books, as well as the covers.

I offered children the following strategies for deciding on their cover illustrations.

1. Close your eyes and think about your story. Try to see a picture in your mind that shows an important part of your story. You can put that illustration on your cover.

2. Look through the book and choose one of the most important parts. Make an illustration of that part for your cover.

3. Look at your title. Use the title as an image for your cover illustration.

Mathematics

GRAPHING

I often asked children to collect, tally, and graph information based on their opinions about the fairy tales. Sometimes children colored in bars on a graph to indicate their choices. At other times, they taped or glued cards on a column corresponding to their vote.

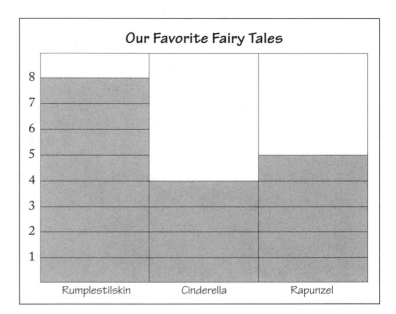

Then we talked about the finished graph.

1. Which fairy tale got the most votes?

2. Which got the least?

3. Which have the same amount?

Then they went on to answer questions that entailed calculations using addition and subtraction.

1. How many children chose *Rumplestiltskin* and *Rapunzel* all together?

2. How many more children chose *Rumplestiltskin* than *Rapunzel*?

Sometimes the children posed their own questions based on the data. They then presented those questions for classmates to answer. Children worked with partners, or in small groups, or as a whole class. Overall, I was pleased that children created their own uses for the information they collected.

WHOLE NUMBER CONCEPTS/PROBLEM SOLVING

We also made use of the many references to number and quantity in the fairy tales. For example, when we read that Briar Rose was to sleep for 100 years, our math lesson focused on how many months, weeks, and days she slept. We also figured out how old Briar Rose would have been when she awoke. (This fit in with the mathematics syllabus on units of measurement, changing the unit of measurement, understanding the concept of multiplication, and developing calculator skills.)

On one occasion, I stated a year in which Briar Rose may have been born. "If she slept for 100 years, in what year would she awake?" I asked. In this way we worked on problem solving and addition.

On other occasions, I pointed out on what page a story began and on what page it ended. The class then calculated how many pages I was going to read in all.

MEASURING TIME

→ If it takes me one minute to read a page, how many minutes will it take for me to finish this story?

→ If it is 9:30 a.m. now, at what time will I be finished?

→ If we finish at 9:40 a.m., and art class is at 10:00 a.m., how many minutes will we have to write before art class?

Social Studies

DEFYING STEREOTYPES

By discussing the stories and the choices characters made, children talked in class about issues of fairness or ethical choices. They also understood that life does not necessarily imitate art. For example, they understood that stepmothers have a range of personality traits (they're not all mean, as in the Grimms' tales). They understood that men and women have different levels of aggression, and that males and females can help each other.

By examining issues through fairy tales, the children were now examining the same issue in their own lives. Nobody could ever again make a statement in my class that "Boys can't..." or "Girls can't..." without a chorus of rebuttals from the other students. The fact that other people's lives were as unique as their own was also coming through.

HISTORY

We discussed how the Grimms recorded the fairy tales, instilling their own personal values as well as the values of their own time and place, over 150 years ago. Social studies talks focused on how the opportunities and roles for men and women have changed over the years. The children developed a sense of history and recognized that things change over time.

GEOGRAPHY

By locating on a globe or map each writer's or storyteller's country of origin, the children gained an excellent sense of world geography and a sense of the cultures of different civilizations.

Art

MAKING MASKS

Art projects were ongoing. At the start of the unit, for example, the children made papier-mâché masks of their fantasy self-portraits—masks that depicted a character the children would like to be. We used corrugated cardboard which I had cut into strips about two inches wide. After softening the cardboard by pressing all around it, the children helped each other wrap the strips around their faces to measure the circumferences of their heads.

They then cut off the extra cardboard and taped the ends together to form the shapes and sizes of their faces. An additional strip of corrugated cardboard was taped to fit

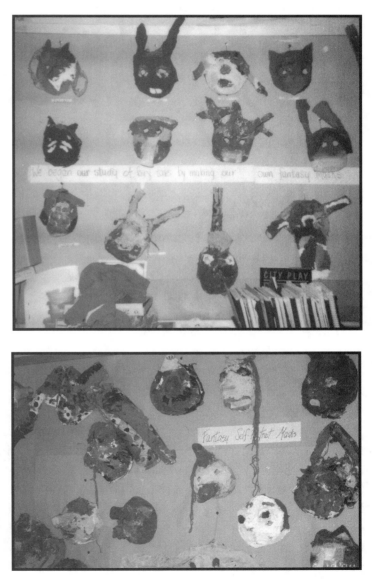

across each child's forehead and attached to the first strip with masking tape.

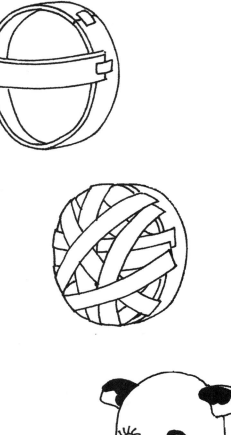

Children stuffed their masks with crumpled newspaper. The next step was to cover the front of the structure with strips of newspaper dipped in a mixture of wheat paste and water. The newspaper strips were applied across the mask until it was covered with about three layers of paper.

When the maskes were dry, children added hair and features by taping on twisted newspaper, yarn, cardboard and various found objects. This was made more permanent by adding a layer of papier-mâché to the newly taped objects. When this was dry as well, the children removed the newspaper stuffing. I cut out the eyes of the masks with a box-cutter knife and the children painted their masks with tempera paint.

The project helped develop children's small motor skills, and of course, their imaginations.

MURALS

We also created large murals of different geographic areas. This helped the children to identify and remember the places of origin of the various stories. It also led us into a study of the animal life that exists in different parts of the world.

We used a multimedia approach. The children started by deciding what color the background of each mural should be, based on the terrain we were depicting. They glued tissue paper onto a large piece of brown paper to form the background of the mural. I encouraged them to overlap the tissue paper. When the glue dried, they used paintbrushes dipped in plain water or in water with a touch of tempera paint added, to paint over the tissue paper. Since this tissue paper bleeds, the result was somewhat unexpected, but always beautiful.

After research, the next step was for each child to draw, on an individual sheet of drawing paper, an animal that lived in the area. Children colored their animals with pencil, then with Craypas™. Youngsters were encouraged to use nature magazines, encyclopedias, atlases, and other resources to help them visualize their animals. They then cut out their animal drawings and glued them onto the mural.

The finished murals decorated our classroom for the rest of the year. They allowed for imaginative trips around the world.

Drama

Drama was an integral part of the year's work. Every story was dramatized during the second reading. The actors performed on our meeting area rug while the other students—the audience—sat around the rug. I narrated, and during the course of the study, each student had the opportunity to play several roles. To be fair, I kept track of how many times each child performed, since most were very eager to perform as often as possible.

It was rewarding for me to witness the children's willingness to play parts with which they did not originally identify. I told them, "A good actor is one who plays his or her part well. The best actors can play a variety of parts well. Remember, the part you play need not be anything like your own character. You just need to do a good job with it."

In this way, students learned to put themselves in another's shoes. By the end of the year, every child felt comfortable role-playing for an audience.

They also learned how to give constructive critiques of each other's performances. I provided the following guidelines.

Critiquing Performances:

    1. Explain what you saw.

    2. Describe what you liked about a particular performance and why.

Students were also given clear guidelines about what it means to be an audience. I told them, "In any performance, the audience is equally as important as the performer. No matter how well the actor does his or her job, it will only feel successful if the audience is paying attention and is involved in the work. The audience needs to do its job, as well as the performers doing theirs."

Both audience and actors took my advice. The audience loved watching their classmates act out the now familiar parts. Dramatization brought the stories to life for the class and helped their recall, understanding, and analysis.

Dance

While our dramatizations of fairy tales were based on literal readings of the tales, our original dances portrayed abstract interpretations. When children found abstract messages in stories, we used dance as one way to express them.

Photo by Veronica Gallea

72

MIRRORING

One of the fables we read was *Little Blue and Little Yellow* by Leo Lionni. In this story, blobs of color are the characters. When two best friends, Little Blue and Little Yellow, spend the day playing together, their colors merge, becoming green. Some children thought the author's message was: Sometimes you can feel so close to somebody else that you feel like you are one.

How could children illustrate this through dance? We tried mirroring. The children were grouped in pairs. Partners faced each other. One dancer from each pair took the leadership role. The leader was to move in place. The other partner, maintaining eye contact, was to mirror the leader's actions. After a few minutes, the leadership and follower roles switched. At its best, the partners appeared to move as one.

The children came to the conclusion that this exercise worked best when their movements were slow and continuous. I played slow, meditative music to inspire these movements.

Students were also instructed to try moving at different levels (high, medium, and low), and to move different body parts (head, fingers, feet, torsos, and so on). As they became more comfortable, I told them to try moving nonsymmetrically, that is, move the two sides of the body differently from each other.

SPINNING

We interpreted spinning in two ways. After reading *Rumplestiltskin*, in which the girl must spin straw into gold, the class experimented with spinning of a different sort. They listed all the body parts on which they thought *they* could spin, including the levels (high, medium, low), and the speeds (slow, medium, fast). Using music by Steve Reich and Johann Sebastian Bach (fugues), we created a dance of solo- and group-spinning movements.

PORTRAYING EMOTIONAL QUALITIES THROUGH MOVEMENT

When dancing the part of Rumplestiltskin, the children used movement to express the qualities of anger and frustration. For this, I used music by Modest Mussorgsky ("Night on Bald Mountain"). The children used large elastic bands to create a calm group dance about weaving straw into gold.

Music

LISTENING AND DANCING

I brought a variety of music tapes to class. The children listened to and then helped select music that they thought best expressed the qualities they wanted to express in their fairy tale dance pieces. In this way they were exposed to a variety of music from different times and places. They learned musical pieces by creating dances to them.

STRUCTURE AND SONG

An aid to the understanding and appreciation of music is the ability to see underlying structure. The extended work we had done in clarifying the structure of fairy tales led to an analysis of form and structure in other kinds of work.

Our day always began with a song. I would write the Song of the Day on chart paper. Then I would sing it to the students or they would listen to it on a tape. They would silently read the lyrics from the chart while listening. We would then discuss the structure of the song in terms of chorus and verse, and the shape of the melody. Then they sang.

Since children had become conscious of gender equity, they often remarked on songs that they felt were stereotypical or biased in gender depictions, such as "Georgie Porgie" and "What Are Little Girls Made of?" Applications to popular songs could easily follow.

Science

As mentioned earlier, children researched the animals that live in the settings of particular stories. This led to animal classification and studies of animal habitats. We also took field trips to zoos and museums. The animal murals revealed the students' interest and research.

AN INQUIRY APPROACH

Finally, the kind of analysis of text that we undertook within this study—looking for patterns, comparing and contrasting variations on a theme, keeping records of our findings, continually questioning the whys and wherefores, and finding new solutions to problems—was actually in the form of an inquiry and a model for future work.

CHAPTER 7

What's Next?

A Shared Journey

 It's hard to say who benefited more from the three years of research and application on fairy tales—me or my students. I know that it was a shared journey in which we all became more critical in our thinking and more humanistic in our outlook. I experience great pleasure when parents of my former students relay to me anecdotes about the ways their children are applying some of our work even years later. Patrick C.'s mother told me a story of how, during a conversation about great men, Patrick piped up, "Well, what about the women?" And Heather B.'s mother told me that Heather's grandfather still treasures his granddaughter's story in which he is portrayed as an example of one kind of strength.

I think that this unit helped my students and me to appreciate the need to look at people as individuals, and to avoid generalizing about them because of their association with a group. When we read books, watched movies, sang songs, or looked at ads, we discussed which characters were realistic and which were merely stereotypes. Rather than closing off to the commercial culture that sometimes surround us, we looked at work critically and were not necessarily swayed by hidden and obvious agendas.

Practice in critical thinking opened up the students' world and my own. Our intellectual appetites became greater as we looked at and evaluated more work. Not only did we critique, but we also sought to understand why things were presented as they were. And we discussed how we might do things differently. My students knew that, by writing their own thoughtful fairy tales, they already had.

Approach and Application

I sincerely hope that the work we've done can serve as a model for other teachers. I would like to emphasize that the approach I used can be applied to other areas of study. I suggest the following techniques and include an example of how I used it with other material.

> **1. Look at the original material (stories, advertisements, etc.) to find values it may be promoting.**

While the focus of this book was on depictions of males and females in the Grimms' books, a subsequent class of mine studied Jean de Brunhoff's *Babar* books. We noted that Babar was elected king in *The Story of Babar* after he learned to be more "civilized" by traveling to Europe. It appeared that the author did not appreciate Babar's native culture.

2. Find similar patterns in related material.

We next looked at the *Travels of Babar* by the same author and noted that native Africans were pictured as cannibals. This further confirmed our feeling that the author did not appreciate, and therefore stereotyped, a culture different from his own.

3. Research contextual explanations for the promotion of particular values.

We learned that these books were written in 1931 and 1932 respectively, when French colonialism was strong in parts of Africa.

4. Question and critique those values.

We questioned the use of stereotypes in the stories. We spoke of the fact that the author was showing lack of understanding.

5. Study alternative models.

We went to the Metropolitan Museum of Art and the American Museum of Natural History to look at wonderful cultural artifacts of Native African cultures. We read folklore from cultures in Africa. We saw evidence of these cultures that defied stereotyping. We also read *Babar* books by other authors and realized we could show other perspectives while using the same characters.

6. Create an original work that provides personal alternatives.

Children wrote original *Babar* books in which their own perspectives shone through.

Though value systems change through history and cultures, many older, culturally significant literary works, like fairy tales, still deserve to be read and savored. Using this approach, the original work lives on, while children engage in critical thinking, creative thinking, and in values clarification as teachers help them with those tasks.

BIBLIOGRAPHY

Books Cited in the Text

Carle, Eric. *Treasury of Classic Stories for Children.* New York: Orchard, 1988

de Brunhoff, Jean. *The Story of Babar.* New York: Random House, 1933. Translated from French original published in 1931.

de Brunhoff, Jean. *The Travels of Babar.* New York: Random House, 1934. Translated from French original published in 1932.

Hastings, Selina. *Sir Gawain and the Loathly Lady.* New York: Mulberry Books, 1987

Lionni, Leo. *Frederick's Fables: A Leo Lionni Treasury of Favorite Stories.* New York: Pantheon Books, 1985

Pasamanick, Judith. *Favorite Fables of Aesop.* Cleveland: Modern Curriculum Press, 1991

Phelps, Ethel Johnston. *Tatterhood and Other Tales.* New York: The Feminist Press, 1978

Seuss, Dr. *Green Eggs and Ham.* New York: Random House, 1960

Seuss, Dr. *Hop on Pop.* New York: Random House, 1963

Seuss, Dr. *Horton Hatches the Egg.* New York: Random House, 1940

Seuss, Dr. *Horton Hears a Who!* New York: Random House, 1954

Seuss, Dr. *How the Grinch Stole Christmas.* New York: Random House, 1957

Seuss, Dr. *McElligot's Pool.* New York: Random House, 1947

Seuss, Dr. *Oh, The Places You'll Go!* New York: Random House, 1990

Seuss, Dr. *Six by Seuss.* New York: Random House, 1991

Seuss, Dr. *Yertle the Turtle and Other Stories.* New York: Random House, 1950

Steig, William. *Amos and Boris.* New York: Farrar, Strauss and Giroux, 1971

Steig, William. *Dr. DeSoto.* New York: Farrar, Strauss and Giroux, 1982

Yolen, Jane. *Sleeping Ugly.* New York: Scholastic, Inc., 1992

Zipes, Jack. *The Brothers Grimm: From Enchanted Forest to the Modern World.* New York: Routledge, 1988

Zipes, Jack. *The Complete Fairy Tales of the Brothers Grimm.* New York: Bantam Books, 1987

Zipes, Jack. *Don't Bet on the Prince: Contemporary Feminist Fairy Tales in North America and England.* New York: Routledge, 1989

FURTHER READING FOR TEACHER RESEARCH

Botigheimer, Ruth. *Grimms' Bad Girls and Bold Boys: The Moral and Social Vision of the Tales.* New Haven: Yale University Press, 1987

Kohl, Herbert. *Should We Burn* Babar? *Essays on Children's Literature and the Power of Story.* New York: New Press, 1995

McGlathery, James M., ed. *The Brothers Grimm and Folktale.* Chicago: University of Illinois Press, 1988

Sale, Roger. *Fairy Tales and After: From Snow White to E. B. White. Cambridge*: Harvard University Press, 1975

Tatar, Maria. *Off With Their Heads! Fairy Tales and the Culture of Childhood.* Princeton: Princeton University Press, 1993

Tatar, Maria. *The Hard Facts of the Grimms' Fairy Tales.* Princeton: Princeton University Press, 1987

Warner, Marina. *From the Beast to the Blonde: On Fairy Tales and Their Tellers.* New York: Farrar, Straus and Giroux, 1995 (first American edition)

Yolen, Jane. *Touch Magic: Fantasy, Faerie and Folklore in the Literature of Children.* Philomel Books: New York, 1981

Zipes, Jack. *Breaking the Magic Spell: Radical Theories of Folk and Fairy Tales.* London: Heinemann, 1979

Zipes, Jack. *Fairy Tales and the Art of Subversion: The Classical Genre for Children and the Process of Civilization.* New York: Methuen, 1983

Zipes, Jack. *The Trials and Tribulations of Little Red Riding Hood: Versions of the Tale in Socio-Historical Context.* London: Heinemann, 1982

Zipes, Jack. *Fairy Tale as Myth, Myth as Fairy Tale.* Lexington, Kentucky: University Press of Kentucky, 1994

RECOMMENDED ADDITIONAL FAIRY TALE COLLECTIONS

Carter, Angela, ed. *The Old Wives Fairy Tale Book.* New York: Pantheon Books, 1990

Minard, Rosemary, ed. *Womenfolk and Fairy Tales.* Boston: Houghton Mifflin, 1975

Phelps, Ethel Johnston, ed. *The Maid of the North : Feminist Folk Tales from Around the World.* New York: Holt, Rinehart and Winston, 1981

Yolen, Jane. *Favorite Folktales from Around the World.* New York: Pantheon Books, 1986

Yolen, Jane. *The Moon Ribbon and Other Tales.* New York: Crowell, 1976

Zipes, Jack, ed. *Spells of Enchantment: The Wondrous Fairy Tales of the Western World.* New York: Penguin Books, 1991

Zipes, Jack, ed. *The Outspoken Princess and the Gentle Knight.* New York: Bantam Books, 1994